April 2017

Happy Easter, Henry, love from
Ken & Carolin

Alfie
in the garden

Debi Gliori

BLOOMSBURY

LONDON NEW DELHI NEW YORK SYDNEY

Can you see Alfie?

Yes, here he is!
He's helping Mama-Bun in the garden.

Look! Alfie's going exploring deep in the jungle.

Ooooh . . . what's in there?
Be careful, Alfie!

Watch out, everyone!

Alfie is a bouncing, pouncing lion.

What's that splishy-sploshy sound?

It's an Alfie-elephant, trying out his trunk!

Eek! Alfie is a rainstorm, sprinkling all his friends.

Listen! Can you hear that?
Alfie is a summer breeze, wafting through the grasses.

SWISH-SWASH,
SWISH-SWASH.

What a huge jungle! What a brave explorer!
But now it's time for a rest.

Alfie is a little bird,
flying home to his nest.

What's Alfie doing now?

He's helping Mama-Bun have a nap.
Cuddle up, Alfie.

What a busy morning!

For all little bunnies
with big imaginations

Bloomsbury Publishing, London, New Delhi, New York and Sydney

First published in Great Britain in 2014 by Bloomsbury Publishing Plc
50 Bedford Square, London, WC1B 3DP

This paperback edition first published in 2015

A CIP catalogue record for this book is available from the British Library

ISBN 978 1 4088 3951 5 (HB)
ISBN 978 1 4088 3952 2 (PB)

Printed in China by C&C Offset Printing Co Ltd, Shenzhen, Guangdong

1 3 5 7 9 10 8 6 4 2

www.bloomsbury.com

All papers used by Bloomsbury Publishing are natural, recyclable products
made from wood grown in well-managed forests.
The manufacturing processes conform to the environmental regulations of the country of origin

BLOOMSBURY is a registered trademark of Bloomsbury Publishing Plc